I dedicate this book to Mom and Dad. Some of my earliest memories are of reading great books. A love of reading is a wonderful gift.

Patrick Words

I dedicate this book to my mother, who brought home rolls of paper for me when I was a kid, and always encouraged me to keep drawing.

Anita

FROGBURPS

Published by Stirling Bay
ISBN: 978-0-9938503-7-0

Written by Patrick S. Stemp
Illustrated by Anita Soelver

The Lonely SN❄WFLAKE

Written by Patrick S. Stemp
Illustrated by Anita Soelver

Visit us at:

www.frogburps.com

Snowflake was falling through the air.
She was surrounded by other snowflakes,
but she was lonely.

None of the other snowflakes looked like her.

She wanted to find another snowflake that looked just like her, so she could have a friend.

Maybe there was a snowflake like her somewhere else in the sky.

She asked another snowflake, "Have you seen a snowflake that looks like me so I can be friends with her?"

The other snowflake said, "No, but we can be friends. We are both made from water."

Snowflake said, "Thank you, but I will keep looking for a snowflake that looks like me."

She flew through the sky, still looking for a friend.

She asked another snowflake. "Have you seen a snowflake that looks like me? I would like to have a friend."

The other snowflake said, "No, but I can be your friend. We are both cold. BRR!"

Snowflake said, "No thank you. I will keep looking for a friend who looks like me."

She kept falling and flying, looking for a friend who looked like her.

She asked another snowflake, "Have you seen a snowflake that looks like me? I am looking for a friend."

The other snowflake said, "Sorry. We all look different. But we are both falling from the sky. We can fall together and be friends."

Snowflake was sad. She was starting to think
that she would never have a friend that looked
just like her.

She flew to another part of the sky. She asked another snowflake, "Have you seen a snowflake that looks like me who can be my friend?"

The other snowflake said, "You will never find another snowflake just like you. But it looks like you already have some friends. Look behind you."

Snowflake turned around and saw that the other snowflakes were following her.

The first snowflake said, "We are all made from water, we can be friends."

The third snowflake said, "We are all falling from the sky together. We can be friends"

The second snowflake said, "We are all cold, we can be friends."

The last snowflake said, "Even though we all look different, we are the same in other ways. We can all be friends."

Snowflake was glad that the other snowflakes wanted to be her friend even though she did not look like them.

They danced in the wind together as they fell through the sky.

They laughed and played and Snowflake forgot  about finding a friend who looked exactly like her.

The author
Patrick S. Stemp

Patrick loves words and telling stories. He writes for both adults and children. Creating for children allows him to share fun and funny stories with young people, and to work with an amazing illustrator to share their vision of a world that will excite and entertain.

The illustrator
Anita Soelver

Anita works full time as a freelance illustrator. She has a strong passion for children related projects, so she was all over it when Patrick suggested that they should team up to create children's books together.

Leave us a review!

Thank you so much for reading our book. We hope you enjoyed it.

It would mean so much to us, if you would leave us a review.

www.frogburps.com/reviewsnowflake

Join our newsletter!

Want to know when our next book comes out?

www.frogburps.com/newsletter

Visit us at:

www.frogburps.com

The End

Find coloring pages with
Snowflake and her new friends
at www.frogburps.com